The Reckoning

A StarSoldier Chronicle

C.R. Coyne

Table of Contents

Feedback

Please leave honest feedback.
Your opinion is important to me!

Also By CR Coyne

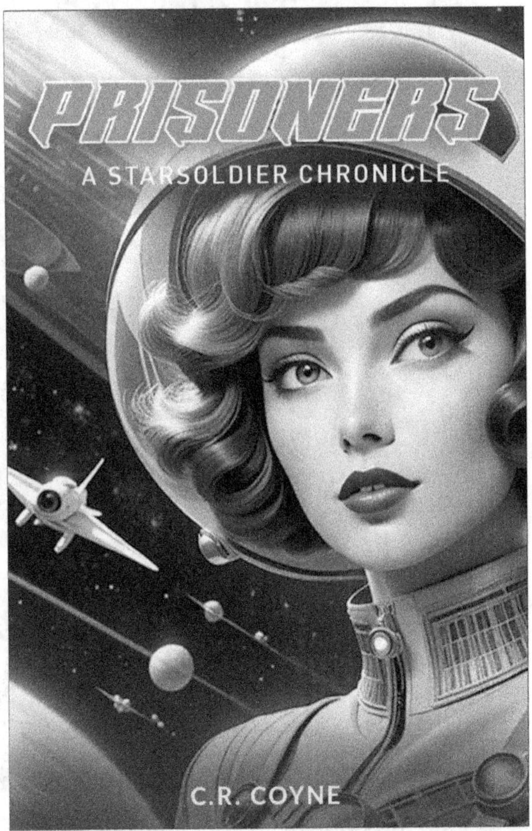

Regulus V was a colony of eight billion humans, rich and comfortable in their adopted home. Great place to visit. But when the entire system becomes a wasteland the StarSoldiers must face an ancient evil as old as the stars themselves and stop it before more die!

Buy your copy today!

Also By CR Coyne

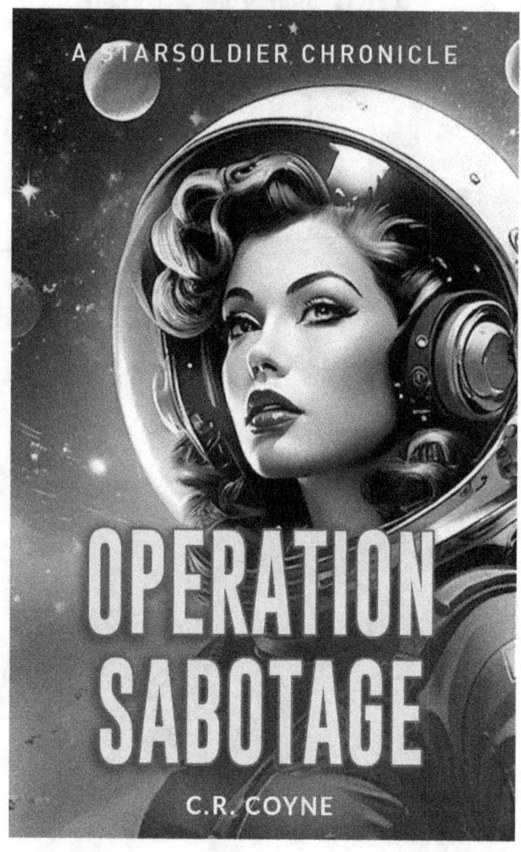

It's just a routine pick up mission. In and out in a few hours no contact with the natives. But the beautiful world of Topaz isn't anymore. Now Yaz and the squad must try and save an entire planet. But if that's not enough first they have to save themselves!

Buy your copy today!

Also By CR Coyne

The squad gets an unexpected camping vacation on a primordial planet, while the Mohawk hangs useless in space.   And every minute is a fight against the cold and the huge hungry wildlife all without weapons. But when the squad finds castaways being used as slaves by a ruthless band of pirates the StarSoldiers do what they do best, even the odds. But how do you fight high tech with sticks and stones?

When the Buy your copy today!

Galactic Area of Human Sphere

Star Map of Notable Sites

History of the Mohawk Tribe

The Mohawk are traditionally the keepers of the Eastern Door of the Iroquois Confederacy, also known as the Six Nations Confederacy or the Haudenosaunee Confederacy. Our original homeland is the north eastern region of New York State extending into southern Canada and Vermont. Prior to contact with Europeans the Mohawk settlements populated the Mohawk Valley of New York State. Through the centuries Mohawk influence extended far beyond their territory and was felt by the Dutch who settled on the Hudson River and in Manhattan. The Mohawks' location as the Iroquois nation closest to Albany and Montreal, and the fur traders there, gave them considerable influence among the other Tribes. This location has also contributed directly to a long and beautifully complicated history.

In the 1750s, to relieve crowding at Kahnawake and to move closer to the Iroquois homeland, the

French Jesuits established a mission at the present site on the St. Regis River. The Mohawk people had continually used this site at the confluence of the St. Lawrence River Valley as part of our fishing and hunting grounds prior to the building of the first church. "Akwesasne" as it is known today, translates roughly to "Land where the partridge drums" has always been a prime location due to the confluence of several small rivers and the St. Lawrence River.

The Reckoning

A Starsoldiers Chronicle

C.R. Coyne

"It just seems like everything is trying to kill you...it's not. It IS going to kill you."—Sergeant Galicky
Advice *for Starsoldier Survival Class 102A page 81*

Jess Yeldon licks her pretty lips looks out of the clearforce panels and shakes her long red braids. "I hate space battles..."

I cheerfully pipe up, "this isn't a combat op. We get close check it out and report. In and out no killing along the way." I thought that was quite logical a response.

Jess has different ideas, she just shakes her head again and repeats, "I hate space battles."

Murphy steps onto the bridge with a crisp clean uniform and attitude and we snap to attention. He takes a peek out the clearforce panels for himself, shakes his head, and mutters, "I hate space battles."

I roll my eyes saying "geez! Doesn't anyone have faith in Earth Intel?"

Dutch tips my hat off my head and asks "do you?"

I pick my cap off the deck take a look at the menacing shape just outside the window and decide I don't. Murphy clears his throat and we all stand rigid and ready for the briefing.

"Earth Intel wants us to give a complete outside report on the object. Next, we enter said object and give a complete report on that. That is all."

"Well, at least the briefing is short." I then ask "does Earth have any information on that thing?"

"Good question corporal, yes they do. It's here. Now get to work." Murphy says to me and I jump to realizing any more questions will only get me cleaning induction jets with my toothbrush. So I sit at my console and start to run a series of scans using every wave band of light known to man. After two hours of steady work, I lean back in my chair with a harrumph and ponder the readings. Or in this case lack of readings. Murphy paces back and forth from one station to the other waiting for one of us to give him something useful. But the bridge stays absolutely silent. I finally decide that cleaning induction jets is better than this and pipe up, "I'm not getting a thing on composition. According to my readings that thing is not there."

"I am getting nothing as vell," Says Dutch the frustration in her voice. "This, this," and to add emphasis to her statement she starts to shove her hand at the clearforce panel in front of her "thing isn't real. I can't even tell you how big it is." My boss looks back at the object and starts to scratch his beard. He's been trying to grow the damn thing for two weeks but he hasn't gotten past stubble at this point. And it makes him look like Poncho Villa.

"How did Earth even know this thing was here?" Yeldon pipes up. A good question.

"Tramp freighter spotted it and reported the object to Finale," Sarge says as he keeps looking at the plates.

Looking over at Striker he cocks his head but Marko just shrugs his shoulders. "I wouldn't even recommend trying to land on it. I mean we might step out into open space." With that pleasant thought, Marko falls silent.

"I'm open to suggestions," Murphy says and Yeldon perks up.

"We could fly around it if nothing else we could just keep track of how far we go around it. There's size. The holo-cameras are useless, I've been snapping away at it for two hours and I have exactly zero useable shots..."

"Good idea Yeldon, suit up," Sarge says nodding.

"That's vhat you get for vulentteering informations," Dutch says a twinkle in her eye as Yeldon heads to the launch bay. Girls can be really mean.

In a few minutes, we see the two man gig start its slow progression around the long equator of the thing, for lack of a better term. The thing is hardly round. I keep my eyes glued to my panels as the gig worms its way around. I set a clock timer and using a base of Yeldon's speed I start to figure a few things out. All of which ends up in a whistle escaping my lips as she crawls at full speed back to its starting point. "That thing is twenty miles in radius," I report then start to watch as Yeldon starts to fly a circuit around the poles. I have a hunch and as she rounds the north pole I nod my head. "Twenty miles right on the button."

The speaker crackles to life and Yeldon's voice comes over, "how big?" Because of my answer she gives her own whistle and then says, "it is pitted and damaged in many areas. All impact damage. My guess is this thing has been out here a long, long, time."

"Is your impression we are dealing with a real object or a holo?" That's Sarge trying to figure out his next move.

"I've seen better holos than this. No, I hate to say this but It's..."

"Yeldon?" I call into my pick-up and then shout Yeldon!" I start to adjust madly and I can hear the rest of the squad doing the same thing. Murphy comes over calmly and looks over my readings. I blink in confusion and look up at Sean, "she's gone. I can't find a single trace."

II

The light was powerful and even through tightly closed eyes was too bright. Yeldon feels the control readings of the gig by touching each display. The gig no longer had an independent motion that she could tell by the seat of her pants. She reads the atmospheric gauge carefully with her fingers twice and wherever she was had a breathable atmosphere. But rather than trusting to luck, she pulls her helmet over her head pops open the canopy of the gig, and steps out on a hard flat surface. The light suddenly dims to a point where she can open her eyes, there are still circles of intense light still floating in her eyes but it's better. Feeling around her body she detects no wounds except a sore spot on her left arm. She waits until her eyes clear and she starts doing simple arithmetic, "I must be inside the object." She says and looks around at the rusted half ruins of an interior bay. The place hadn't been cleaned or even new for hundreds of years. Much of the equipment was familiar much to her surprise. She walks over and pulls out some fiber optic cable from the wall. The filaments still glow even though the information they carry is not going anywhere. Lights adorn some of the walls with simple control panels.   All are labeled but the language is indecipherable, if it is a language. That was Dutch's job to figure out. "First things first," she says and heads back to the gig and gives it a full inspection.   The little craft seemed right enough. Pulling out the survival pack she sits down and clips odds and sods to her utility belt. Taking a large bite out of one of the amorphous sticks labeled 'Dinner' she makes a sour face and shoves it back into its pack. Thinking better of it she says "Sergeant Galicky wouldn't approve," and starts to munch on the bar unable to think of it as anything but sawdust.

After her meal, she starts to move around what she presumes is a bay and then using the only useable door heads out into the interior of the giant twenty mile long craft. All the passageways are cluttered with equipment, fallen girders, and broken glass nearly choking out the passageway. Picking up a piece of glass she thinks, "so much for advanced beings. This thing is as primitive as you can get in space travel." A red band of color painted on the floor attracts her attention next and she follows until she reaches a red door. Only red door she'd seen. The star symbol on the door is conventional and almost, well, human. The door grinds open fighting every inch of the way until its opening is large enough for a person to pass through if they're thin. Stepping inside Yeldon finds a strange circular room dominated by some kind of tripod with a huge glass ball in the middle of it. The ball has a faint glow buried deep within it that pulses slowly. The walls have some kind of design, the regular patterns look a great deal like writing. "Where's Dutch when I need her?" Grouses Yeldon as she looks around the small chamber careful not to touch anything. Putting her hands on her hips she says out loud, "now what?"

At the sound of her voice soft lights steadily brighten until the chamber is bathed in yellow light like a romantic restaurant might have. From deep within the glass ball a booming and disconcertingly human voice speaks in basic..."Justify yourself..." If there was room Jess would have jumped a mile. Backing slowly away from the voice slash glowing ball thing she looks carefully at it while drawing her service pistol. The ball waits a few moments and then again demands "justify yourself..."

"I...I don't understand the question." Jess says while watching for any sign the ball is about to do something aggressive.

The ball sits quietly waiting for an answer saying nothing and doing even less as it just pulses away. The thing is not AI, just a voice response system. Probably asking for some kind of password or some such primitive computing silliness.   Still, Yeldon would have to figure out how to communicate with the thing if she were to get off this monster. So with the spirit of the old college try she asks "who are you?" The ball crackles and then tries to speak but ends up sounding like a broken data disc on too low a speed.   Getting more forceful when she realizes the thing will speak, or try to anyway she commands "state your purpose."

"I am Oracle. My purpose: to render assistance and guidance..." the rest of the answer gets lost as it winds through the machine's data banks only to be garbled through the speaker.

"I must leave this vessel, how do I do that from my present location?"

"Justify yourself and enter the key code." The Machine answers assertively and Jess just rolls her eyes.

"Haven't you people ever heard of retinal scans?"

"Not used for..." It starts out but with a quick "shut up" from Yeldon the machine quiets down waiting.

"Oracle is there any intelligent life on this ship?" Jess asks but the machine stays mute. Asking a second time yields the same result. As little as the machine has given her Yeldon decides it's better than what she started with. One thing was for sure, the ship was of human design. But who of the myriad human planets out there made it is uncertain. Even less certain is why. She'd just have to roam around the wreck and see if she could find some evidence of the makers. The machine had spoken in an archaic dialect but it was still basic alright. The fact the machine spoke basic meant something important. But only if she could tie it into who made the thing. Leaving the place Yeldon has a choice, follow the red stripe back to the gig or keep looking around. Both prospects had drawbacks to be sure. If she roamed around a twenty mile long ship how long would it take for her to get lost? If she returned to the gig how long until Sarge and the gang found her? She had already given up on opening the huge bay doors. Standing in the middle of her dilemma she turns left plunging deeper into the giant craft and hopefully some answers.

I look over every instrument I have and come up with the same answers I started out with. Rubbing my eyes I pull away from the screen and stare at the thing with anger then fascination as I start to just stare taking in every part of the supership. I hear Striker throw off his data goggles in frustration and stalk out off the bridge. He should ask to be excused but with the mood he's in it's probably better to just let him go. I watch him leave then go back to my clearforce panel. Dutch asks "are you planning to stare it to death?"

I shrug my shoulders and watch the thing a little more than say, "nothing else works." As I look a few thoughts begin to pervade my thinking. I start looking at specific areas of the ship.

Sergeant Murphy comes over looks at my panel then murmurs, "it could be centuries before we catch up to those guys."

That's when the penny that's been balancing on the edge of my consciousness finally drops my way and I ask, "who says?"

Murphy blinks and gives me a "remember your protocol," look then expands on his comment. "I'm just saying that thing is mighty advanced. Well beyond us."

I look closely at the panel and then say "no it's not. In fact, these shmoes are way behind us. Look at the bell housing for the main thruster assembly. Whoever designed it never heard of Hyper-Theory. And look at the design of the whole ship, no AG none on that ship. They must bounce around like ping-pong balls unless that thing spins while it flies. I know we can't get readings but it just occurred to me that there are lots of things we can't get readings on, like ion typhoons, or Aldeberan Fire Bats even when they're swarming. No sir, it is not advanced. It's just made of something our sensors can't penetrate. And it is old, maybe a couple hundred years." My confidence begins to outstrip my caution and I find myself saying, "I say we land on it. Full up armed and dangerous. Then let's go find Jess and bring her home. There is nothing on that floating junk pile we can't handle, one way or another."

Sergeant Murphy looks me over assessing how much is bravado and how much is well reasoned logic. I don't blame him I'm doing the same thing. But then he nods his head. "Alright people suit up, we're going sightseeing."

IV

Yeldon wanders the deck she's on poking her stubby little nose in every nook and cranny, not that there weren't opportunities to go up or down to other decks. There were plenty. But where she'd end up was another matter. So for now she'll stick to this one floor. Every once in a while she'd walk back to the bay just to make sure she could get back to the gig. After about twelve hours of exploring she decides to take off the helmet and breathe the local political fuel. The air is musty and smells of decay but it's safe enough. Heading in a new direction she follows the deck for almost three miles until she reaches an area that has the odor of cooking fires. The rancid smoke sits just above her on the low ceiling of this part of the ship collecting in a greasy smudge that permeates the whole deck.

Pushing onward curious as to what could have been burning for so long. And come to think about it why Oracle hadn't attempted to put the fire out, supposing of course the machine mind had some way of doing so, didn't. The smoke grows thick and clotted as she rounds several bends and comes face to face with the fires. The small flames have been carefully tended with metal barriers set around the three fires in a ring. Someone had done that, and the whatever it was burning on the stick was very, very new. Striding boldly into the encampment for now Jess was sure that was what this place was she has a look around. Small handmade metal tools lie scattered around rough metal benches that might have been medical bed scanners at one time. Looking around she sees no one but they'd have to come back if only to tend to the fire and grab their tools. Looking over the tools she realizes they're of the most basic types, knives for cutting food, forks made out of Hyper-spanners the ends ripped off to expose the rugged triple tines of the sensors packs. As she looks over the spits in the fire she realizes it's some kind of animal that is cooking. "Probably a parasite like a rat or something akin to that from another planet," she muses out loud. Looking up into the rafters where the ceiling panels have been taken down she freezes. Eyes! About a dozen pairs of eyes watch her every move. Looking closely she sees they are made up of a white orb, an iris, and a pupil. Not much else of the creatures can be seen. Then a rumble shakes the rafters a panel explodes outward crashing onto the deck with a body falling with it. Looking over she sees the shape roll around in pain and goes to him or her. It's hard to tell the tangle of long hair and dirty face and body give nothing away. It moans clearly hurt. Yeldon looks up and sees the rest of the eyes have disappeared. Kneeling next to the mass she pulls out her bioscanner and starts to take a reading. The skeleton and musculature is human no doubt about it, and female judging by the construction of its pelvis. The girl struggles to get up but falls back heavily.

Fixing Yeldon with a direct look the child says "end me quickly, don't eat me live monster."

That stops Jess dead in her tracks, "eat you? I'm not going to eat you. I'm just trying to help. Here this will help with the pain. You broke your shoulder when you fell."

V

We head to the landing craft all suited up and armed to the teeth. Of course, if that thing out there isn't there we'll be well prepared to die in the lonely vacuum of space. Sarge lines us up, more or less, and we snap to attention, again more or less. "Anyone who wants to back out do so now. No ramifications. Every sensor we have says there is nothing there. Maybe they're right." We all stand stalk still and wait for the order to board. Murphy smiles or at least as much as he allows himself when on duty and we file onto the craft. Dutch heads to the front straps in and we lift off.

I think things through and decide to pull rank, "Dutch you stay with the landing craft. Just in case everything else goes south, at least you'll still be here."

"So I can report on the fate of your bodies? Nice thought." She quips.

"No, so we have something to return to outside that ship," I reply then start to dig around my packs making sure I have everything I may need. I have no idea what you take to the ghost ship but I don't want to be out something once I get there. We skim low along the surface of the ancient alien craft looking around trying to find how and where Jess and the gig disappeared. As our eyes skim the surface Striker points out a panel off to our left, flying over to it I can see a seam and what appears to be landing lights now dark. The design is unmistakable and just confirms my hunch that these folks are no great shakes at space travel. Building mighty big? Yes! But the portholes are glass the ship is a patchwork of hull plates fitted together like a giant jigsaw puzzle and even the navigation lights are simple old fashioned LEDs.

Dutch flies us to within ten feet of this apparent hatchway, "are we close to where she disappeared?" I ask Dutch who nods her head. The landing door opens and I with everyone else jump out and fall slash fly to the ship below. The thing is heavy enough to have a slight but useful gravity field of its own. My feet touch the ground to my relief. I hate to admit it but I was kinda expecting to drift off into space as the illusionary ship laughs at me. Walking past the squad I kneel down and look over the controls and I am struck at once how almost human these controls are. Pulling what appears to me as a manual release I pop open not the main hanger door but a small side access door. On the left hand side of the lock is some kind of writing I think.

We pile through the airlock and I manage to open the second door, we're lucky the lock still cycles through and we are admitted into the craft under pressure. First thing I find is the gig settled snugly on its landing pads. What I don't find is Yeldon. But at least we know she is here. Somewhere. And there is a lot of somewhere to search.

"Fourteen point two pounds psi Sarge," says Striker who then giggles and takes his helmet off. For a second I almost jump out of my skin trying to save him from his foolish act only to find him standing there breathing helmet off and smiling at me. Carefully and with a great deal more fear than I will ever admit to, I take my helmet off too. The air is musty and old but it is air.

"What if this thing was made by humans?" I ask no one in particular but I think it's a valid question. Nobody else does they all look at me like I am crazy. But the thought keeps tugging at the back of my skull and raising my hackles. So as I sometimes do I persist in making a fool of myself to my fellow squad mates. "No, I'm not crazy. Look at the controls to this thing. They're all very human and even understandable by just looking at them."

Murphy shakes his head at me and pats my shoulder, "you are right so far. Don't blow it by climbing out on a very thin limb."

"I know this fa-cockamamie thing is human in origin."

Murphy just smiles at me and asks, "okay professor, how do you know that?" He asks indulging my delusion a little longer.

"Because they're looking at us right now," I point and several sets of eyes up in the ceiling work above us stares down. They look hungry. In a flash, they drop down and start to howl like wild animals brandishing old metal tools, some thigh bones of people, anything that will put a dent in your head.

With a unified scream, they charge us crossing the distance between us in nothing flat. But I have my weapon up as does everyone else. We start firing hoping these aren't the only people on this thing. In about two seconds the attacking mob is asleep. I head over check out the bodies and show the results to everyone. Nice to be right, better to be confirmed right by a bio-scanner, and they are human really, really dirty but human.

Striker shakes his head, "look at this place will ya? It's ancient. There aren't any humans that could build like this a thousand years ago."

Murphy clicks on his helmet quad-scanner clacks his tongue and says "I'm still not getting anything. But Yaz I've got to agree with Striker, this thing is old. How did someone build it say one hundred years ago? We can't build it now."

"What you mean to say is we don't want to build it now. Not that we can't. But let's say a colony very far out that lost faster than light might build a generation ship and send it back this way."

"And they did this vhy?" Asks Dutch to which I can only shrug my shoulders. I only have a limited number of answers.

VI

The young woman sits up tests her arm and makes an "O!" with her mouth as she flexes the appendage in wonder. "You must be smart like the others."

Yeldon shrugs and smiles at the gratitude even as she tries to figure out who or what the others might be. At this point Yeldon decides the best thing she can do is try and get the kid to talk and maybe piece together the puzzle this ship represents. "How long have you lived here?"

"You mean how long have I been an underling? Or how long I've been alive."

With a fielder's choice, Yeldon plays it safe "both actually."

"Well, I wasn't always an underling you know. Once when I was young and pretty I lived in the world. But then my owners got tired of me and so here I am. But I've lived on the Life Raft all my life."

"So the underlings are slaves?" Jess asks disturbed by where this conversation is going.

"No man my own another that is a wrong thing. But I was hired by an Other to be his consort. I got to wear pretty clothes and shoes. Real shoes! You know made of soletex, not animal skin. And I got to visit the great houses of the others. It was fun. And if Master pawed me every once and a while, well that was part of the contract."

"Sounds like marriage," Yeldon says wryly as the child's eyes dance. "How old are you?"

"I'm old, almost fifteen. I've been lucky to last this long. Most don't. But maybe you'll buy my contract?" The young woman looks up hopefully.

Yeldon smiles and shakes her head at that, "well, maybe. Have to clean you up first! You're a mess. But first off what's your name?"

"Oh, I don't have nearly enough cred for that! But if you keep me long enough I might earn a name."

"Well, I can't just call you, you. So how about Ophelia?"

The girl's brow wrinkles as she thinks over the name, "well it is not bad. If I call myself Op...O...What is it?"

"Ophelia, she's a famous character in a play." Yeldon provides as the girl's mind works over the name some more.

"Okay if I call myself Ophelia you have to buy me."

"Deal," Yeldon says shoving her hand out toward the girl who grasps the offered hand and giggles. The girl nods and smiles. Wiping the dirt off the child is beautiful thinks Yeldon. But a vague sense of anger overtakes her, but she can't quite put her finger on why. "Now where are these others? How do I get to them?"

The girl gets confused shaking her head, "don't you know how?"

"Nope, I just arrived I have no idea where I am. I was surprised to find anyone alive here."

The new Ophelia's eyes grow huge and unconsciously she backs away from her new not owner and whispers "did you come from the otherside?"

The girls' eyes as big as dinner plates watch Yeldon so closely that Jess is uncomfortable. The answer could change everything between them for better or not at all. The child's reaction was proof of that. And how do you answer a question you don't understand? Fortunately, Jess had a safe enough course, just don't answer. She shrugs smiles pats the rats nest that makes up the girl's hair and shrugs. "How about we head back to my er..." ship, didn't sound like the right thing to say so "house." Would have to do. The young waif takes the offer and nods and Yeldon and her new charge march off away from the cooking fires and rat on a stick cuisine and walk back to the hanger. On arriving Yeldon's heart leaps for joy, someone from the squad has planted a homing flag on her gig. Reaching over she taps the activation node and the small light begins to blink on and off.

"You must be from the otherside. Even the Others don't have doohickeys" Ophelia says pointing at the flag.

VII

We follow a red strip that is painted down the middle of the passageway until we reach a red door. I scan and find traces of Yeldon's DNA on the door and inside the strange round room. The globe in the middle of the room pulses with an inner light but does precious little else. Deciding there is little joy to be gained from here we start to go down the hallway toward the smell of burning meat. Reaching this place we find cooking fires fueled by the flammable guts of the ship. A small group of people again hide in the rafters above us, but our reputation or something prevents them from attacking, they just run away leaving us to their meal. Frankly, they can have it back. Stretching a little further around I find some med-kit waste on the deck, Yeldon was here fixing someone or herself. The amount of blood is minimal so there was no firefight. As we look around a shot rings out which blows just past my ear and buries itself in the bulkhead in front of me. "Halt! By order of the Others, you will be detained."

"Like hell," Striker says and opens fire. The policemen or whatever they are haven't seen a Type-10 in action and as Striker chews through walls, deck plates, and policemen with every shot they don't hesitate to run away. We close into their position and find two dead and a blood trail leading away down the corridor. Murphy pokes his beard around the corner only to have it shot at. Thinking quickly I fumble around my belt for a second and find what I am looking for. Striker wrinkles his nose at me and asks "do you have to use that?" I nod give a terrible grin of a madman and toss the gas grenade. The small tube lands close to the opposition who look at it dumbly but only for two milliseconds then it goes off spraying a noxious tear gas around the place.

"Helmets people." Murphy orders as we listen to the police cough, sputter, and start to cry. We race up and find our antagonists rolling on the floor gasping and wishing they were anywhere in the universe but here. I pat one down and find a small electronic device that must be at least a hundred years old. It's a kind of electric mapping device, while simultaneously I kick his rifle away from him. That thing is a relic too. The man fights feebly as the effects of the gas take him over to grasp his gun then rolls over vomits and passes out. His two comrades don't see suffering together as glamorous and drag themselves away to hide in the endless passages of the ship.

I scroll through the device and shake my head, the thing is just a palm reader that has a map displayed. "They seem to have come from seventy decks straight up."

"Then that's where we need to go," Murphy says just as the homing signal on Yeldon's gig lights up on his HUD. "Yaz go get Yeldon. We're going to search the area a little more catch up and we'll head upstairs." I nod and dog trot back to the bay.

I trudge my way back passing the fires, the campers have left it maybe for good and I find my way to the red stripe. Following that I trace it through piles of junk and wreckage until I make it to the bay. As long as I am pointed in its general direction the homing beckon will ping loudly in my ears. By the time I reach the bay the ping has turned off no longer worried about me finding it. That means it's right in front of me. I twist on the door lock and enter. There I see Yeldon sitting next to the gig with a pile of rags laughing and conversing with it. The rag pile gets one look at me screams grabs Yeldon and tries to haul her away from me. "Othersider!" The rags scream and I realize it's a human that hasn't washed in eighteen or so years. I'd love to say this is the first time I've been screamed at in combat armor. I'd love to, but... Yeldon holds on for dear life to the strange human and starts to calm it. I try to help by taking my helmet off, which only elicits another tirade and screaming until the ragamuffin looks at my face then it stops. "You're too handsome to be an Othersider. Maybe you would buy my contract huh? Or better yet you both could! I can lay out teas, and dinner parties. I look great in green."

I look at Yeldon lost and drowning in incomprehension. She just smiles and says "I'll explain later. Yaz I'd like you to meet Ophelia." I nod politely not seeing the point in introductions at the moment but what the heck.

"She's going to buy my contract if I call myself Ophelia." The rags offer.

"Yeah, I'm sure she will." Looking at Yeldon I roll my eyes "What is it with you and Shakespeare?" Jess only gives me a little smile. At this point, I'm confused beyond my limit for confusion and decide to get back to the problem at hand. "Sarge caught your beacon, we're moving out. We got a map so we're going to follow it up about seventy decks."

Jess turns to the mound, "I want you to stay here."

"Yes, Mistress." The rags say and performs a curtsey rather well. At least now I know the rags are female. "But Mistress what if you don't come back?"

"I'll be back, I promise." Yeldon says and goes into the gig and breaks out her combat gear.

"I didn't know girls could be warriors," Ophelia states then she goes inside the gig sits down, and starts to play with her fingers.

I smirk at Yeldon, "yeah I didn't know girls could be warriors..." I say.

"Watch it Yaz they can also be boxers," Yeldon states flatly to me and I giggle and lead the way. Looking back over my shoulder I see Ophelia peering out of the clearforce at us. She gives me a weak smile then piles out of the gig and runs over to us.

I can see Yeldon trying to contain her anger at being disobeyed so I put a restraining arm on her saying, "not a soldier. Settle down." Jess looks over at me swallows and nods.

"I need to go with you." Ophelia says, "you can beat me if you wish Mistress..." and here memory seems to take over Ophelia for a second. "But you need me. You don't know the Others, they're...dangerous." She says in a small voice.

I take over, "we do need a guide, Jess. We have no idea what we are getting into. If these people are buying and selling each other I...well deceit and violence can't be far behind."

I can see Jess fight the idea not because she's being defied but because she's taken a liking to Ophelia and doesn't want her hurt. "You can't go like that," Yeldon says and Ophelia looks at herself then looks into Jess's eyes. Yeldon takes her hand "C'mon!" and drags us all back to the gig. How I'm going to explain to Sarge we stopped off for a quick bath is beyond me. But stripes or no I don't think I can stop this. Yeldon and Ophelia head back to the gig and Jess pulls out several plastic sheets we use as tent material then she sets up the vaporator which produces water from usable atmosphere attaching some tubing to a makeshift nozzle. I help with the set up then am told to go away or stand guard or something useful besides ogling. Which I do by seeking Murphy and finding him heading back to the gig.

"Where the hell have you been?" He asks and I salute.

"Located Yeldon sir she has a civilian with her. She's..." Okay, son of Aatiq stay calm and report. "She is currently bathing the civilian."

"She's what?" Murphy says and Striker starts to laugh.

"Bathing the civilian sir." It is only now I realize how many induction jets there are onboard the Mohawk. Murphy shakes his head looks me up and down then heads back to the gig as well. "Ummm Sir? Yeldon asked for privacy the civilian is a young woman about fourteen or fifteen something like that."

Murphy turns his eyes on me like I've gone mad, which now that I have time to reflect I must've. Pointing at my shoulder pad Murphy says "forget all about those?" Referring to my stripes. He walks past me. The pressure door to the bay opens and I hear Yeldon shout "Get out you perv!" A second later Murphy comes out red faced. Straightening my indomitable commander says "yes, well we all might profit from a little rest." About an hour later Yeldon and the most beautiful child I have ever seen step out of the bay. Ophelia is dressed in a service jump suit her long blond hair combed out. She has the kind of beauty that does not require makeup and I can't help but wonder what fool would have gotten rid of her.   But there is something in the eyes of this almost woman that makes me want to protect her, she's more child than woman still. Yeldon snaps to and gives a crisp salute.

"Bath time over rifleman?" Murphy asks and Yeldon nods.

"Sir, I truly believe Ophelia can help us. She has told me a great deal about the Others. If we're going up to meet them we better go ready for a fight."

Murphy shakes his head, "why would they want to fight their own kind Yeldon?"

"Sean," My eyes bulge at the breach but Sergeant Murphy just listens more closely to Yeldon not even blinking. "That is just the point. We're not their own kind. Ophelia here was a slave," Ophelia perks up at that, "no I wasn't I was a consort..." Yeldon hushes her with a hand on the girl's arm. "They even have these poor people brainwashed into believing they're not slaves. The Others are a dying group, Sean. This ship you've seen it, it's falling apart. How much longer before everyone on board dies from lack of food, water, or both?"

"How the hell did they build it in the first place? And why?" Striker adds. That come to think about it is the most important question asked so far.

Ophelia brightens up again and offers, "Oh we didn't build it, the Otherside built it. We just live in it now. It's home, now that Colony is gone..." Murphy turns to say something when over his shoulder I see about twenty armed men taking up positions around the bay. I can't figure out how they got in without us hearing them then I see the ropes they slid down on hanging from the ceiling.

In rapid succession twenty more descend and twenty more for good measure. "We are in trouble," I say and drop my rifle to the deck. Everyone else follows suit I look over at Ophelia wide eyed and terrified. I hate to think she's right, but she knows these people better than we do.

VIII

Administrator Kravic looked at the televised capture of the underlings and rubbed his beard. The ones in combat clothing were astonishingly clean and healthy. Taming them would be difficult if not impossible, but still, he liked a challenge. Looking down he sucks in his breath then into the mike and says "bring them to me." He sees the protector nod his assent. The man could not speak to the Administrator that would be a breach of protocol.

Looking over his equipment and training rooms Administrator Kravic plans his campaign.

End

It takes us six hours to make it to deck seventy the entire trip was by stairs the autolifts no longer work. Our captors keep their weapons trained on us the whole time never letting their guard down. If Ophelia is right these are underlings like her. But condition for loyalty they would not betray the Others by us simply talking to them. And with the number of steps we have to surmount I and everyone else is out of breath by the time we make it to the top. As we break away from the stairs bright sunlight from a G-1 star floods the area with yellow warm light. A few spots however I notice are dark, the bulbs must be burned out or some such. Ophelia clings to Yeldon never letting her go. Once in and while I think about breaking out my armor would handle most of the shots these goons would take at me but it's that small other portion that it won't that stops me from trying. I'll wait for a better time. All the people on this deck look almost just the same, tall, blond, clean, and above all well fed. We are marched past them, I notice they hardly bother to look at us. We finally reach a set of gold doors, these slide open and we are ushered into a large round room upon which sits a tripod not unlike the smaller version down below.

Men in white robes sit at a high table and gaze down at us. "Reminds me of my recruiting council," I comment and for a reward, I get a knot on my head as a rifle butt is slammed up against it.

"Justify yourselves!" The glass globe shouts at us, I have no idea what to say so I stay mum and let Murphy carry the water on this one. But he's as confused as I am. Turns out it's Ophelia who comes to our aid.

"We are free underlings, without contract."

"Where do you come from?" The globe asks. Looking over at Yeldon she licks her lips, takes a step forward, and clears her throat. "Uh-oh." I think as I anticipate the next knot on my head from her answer.

"We are from the Otherside..." Jess couldn't have caused a bigger stink if she had tossed a tear gas grenade. The guys at the table jump up and babble, as they make hand gestures toward us to ward off even spirits, is my guess. The armed men back off still holding their weapons on us. Only us simple StarSoldiers stand still, and Ophelia who seems to revel in all this.

One of the table guys handkerchief in hand says "take them to Administrator Kravic at once!" Well, so much for the trial. Now on to the punishment.

We are dragged out of the room and rushed one deck below to a set of rooms. Inside are weird devices and a spider of a man sitting right in the middle of them. I know a torture chamber when I see one. Ophelia knows one too, if she could climb inside Yeldon she would. Her blue eyes bulge in fear and I can see her shoulders shaking.

The little spider looks us over and I'm about to make a comment when he speaks into some kind of ancient pick-up "obvious underling types. Skin tones show inferior breeding, low slopping heads, and dull eyes show signs of sluggish minds. Probably best used in manual or violent labor." He points a bony finger with a nail an inch past the tip at me. "He'll do." Two of the guards grab me and start dragging me to one of the glass boxes kept in the corners of the chamber. It's at this point I decide docile no longer works for me. I twist my wrist and flip my two captors head over heels onto the floor. They roll away and two more guards out of the dozen that stand watching over us start firing at me. The slugs they use shatter on my armor sending splitters all over the room nicking Ophelia's cheek. That's when I really get mad. But it seems I'm not the only one, Yeldon twisting a rifle from the guard next to her blows his guts out and kills with cool efficiency two more Guards as they turn to run. That frees up two more rifles and by now

Striker and Murphy are causing their own special brand of chaos as guards are tossed around the room like rag dolls. Striker grabs up a loose rifle first and starts firing quickly followed by Murphy. I turn to the spider and to my astonishment he just sits passively in the middle of his torture machines waiting the outcome of the battle. By now there is no doubt as to that as over half the guards are lying on the ground bleeding or dead the rest out the door and running for their lives. Things settle down to strange quiet. A huge smile makes its way across Ophelia's face and she turns to the torture master and says "told you they were the real thing."

He nods once and looks us up and down and says "so it would seem darling. And now we have the instrument."

Murphy decides they hung stripes on him for a reason and he looks at his rifle frowns at it gently slings it over his shoulder and says "okay, so do we shoot you and wreck the rest of this nasty little room of yours or do we walk out without a problem from you."

Now that things settle down I get a chance to look at the spider, he bears a striking resemblance to Ophelia down to the shape of his mouth and teeth. That can't be coincidence "you're her father?"

Spider nods then smiles beaming all pride. "She is indeed my daughter. And you, are our deliverers."

Ophelia smiles up at Yeldon, "I never believed we would find you. Only my father and I thought the myths might be true. So we concocted a story and I went to the subfloors to look for you. Now you are the reckoning."

Jess's eyes goggle at Ophelia, being faster than the rest of us right now she asks "Wait a minute you think we are the ones that built this ship, and you've been looking for us for what purpose?"

"To end tyranny, my dear," the man says. "To end the contracts, the privileged few that live here at the top of the world while the rest scramble for crumbs below. My daughter must have told you this world is dying."

Jess shakes her head, "we just sorted guessed at it."

"The texts said you would be wise. Yes, the resources of the ship are running out. The systems that recycle our water, make useable things of waste, the repair systems are all breaking down.

You must destroy the Others then you must guide us to a home."

I take all this in then I say slowly, "we're not the Otherside folks. We did not come from somewhere on this ship, we were sent by our authority to investigate this ship. And last thing on our to-do list is sparking a revolution. Right boss..." I start out but then I catch a glimpse of Murphy, he seems to be listening actually considering. I feel a shot of fear and say, "if we intervene this whole society becomes our problem."

Murphy nods his head sagely then mutters to me "somebody has to take up the problem."

Feedback

Please leave honest feedback.
Your opinion is important to me!

Beta Readers Wanted

My Email

cr.coyne@yahoo.com

Looking forward to hearing from you! Please email your desire to be a beta reader.

Who I am

I love telling stories and the more out of this world the better. I hope you enjoy my musings as much as I enjoy spinning them. I spend my time writing, running my business, riding my bike too fast everywhere and catering to my cat Ares! Oh, and writing.

COPYRIGHT

© copyright C.R. Coyne 2024

Prisoners

A StarSoldier Chronicle

C.R. Coyne

"The night is long that never finds the day."—
William Shakespeare: McBeth

"**I** don't mind telling you I'm scared." She says in hushed tones though the lab is completely soundproof. He looks over at her no expression on his face as he works the strange arrangement of devices in front of him. "I suppose that doesn't mean much to you, having no emotions."

His mouth twists at the jab proving under the cold exterior exists some emotion just buried deep enough he could control it, most of the time. He puts down the alien instrument and turns to face her, for the first time that evening. "I also have qualms about this project regardless of what you may think of my emotional state. But I believe we and I do me we Doctor Xu will make history tonight. I believe there is a purpose in all things, even if we don't immediately see it. You and I finding this place, all this technology from a lost civilization, that must mean something. Shall we begin?"

She looks at his excitement and the desire in his eyes and smiles gently, "why not? History waits for no man, or so I am told."

"You know if this works we'll be able to find out if that is true." He moves the toggle to the right and the small telltale lights up green and the flow of power begins. The subtle glow of the alien device was expected and both scientists smile as their predictions are proven true. While watching they begin to hear the worrying sound of the generator starting to spin faster and faster. That was not supposed to happen. "Shut it off!" Doctor Xu screams as the light from the device becomes unbearable the generator now howling as it tries to give what the device demands. He races around the table toward the generator only to stop, the heat coming from the device is incredible, how it's still functioning is unbelievable. Still, the alien contraption purrs getting brighter, starting to make its own high pitched whistle tearing at their ears until they bleed. "Jonathon!" She screams as the expected gateway opens, she sees the strange shadow begin to emerge from the device. At first, it looked for all the world human. But as extra legs and a tail begin to show it transforms into a nightmare. One claw reaches out to touch a new land. Like a man testing the temperature of water, the thing slowly slips past the energy curtain that separates it from its world into ours. Doctor Xu pushes away her chair and races behind to find Jonathon lying dead on the floor burned to a crisp. She knows it's her death to go on, but scientist that she is, she knows her duty in a failed experiment and pushes past the heat and shimmering energy and yanks the wire shrieking in agony as the alien energy tears at her body burning the flesh from her face and hands.

As the power is cut the thing comes through hefting a strange crystalline hand weapon. It stands there watching the death of the bi-ped. It tests the gravity of this new place rising and falling on all six legs smiles and takes a deep breath of the strange chemical mix, it's foul but breathable. The bi-ped casts one eye on it then exhales and lies limp. It was always so with the first ones. Those that would presume to learn the secrets of the Hota. It walks calmly and snaps the wires back in, after all, what was the use of being alone in a new land?